Stella and Steve travel through Space!

Written by
James Duffett-Smith

Illustrated by
Bethany Straker

Sky Pony Press
New York

"I wish I lived somewhere else," said Stella.
She went over to the shelf and found a book on the solar system.
"I want to live on another planet!" she cried.

"I don't think you'd like living on another planet," Steve said.

"Well, I can't go there," Stella agreed. "Let's go to Venus instead!"

Steve replied, "After the sun and the moon, Venus is the brightest thing in the sky. But it rains acid and is hot and the pressure in the atmosphere would crush you!"

Venus

Stella yelped. "Yikes! That's not a good idea. Hmm. What about Mars?"

"Mars is cold, dead, and lonely," Steve sighed. "Some people thought there could be life there. But if there is, no one has been able to find it yet."

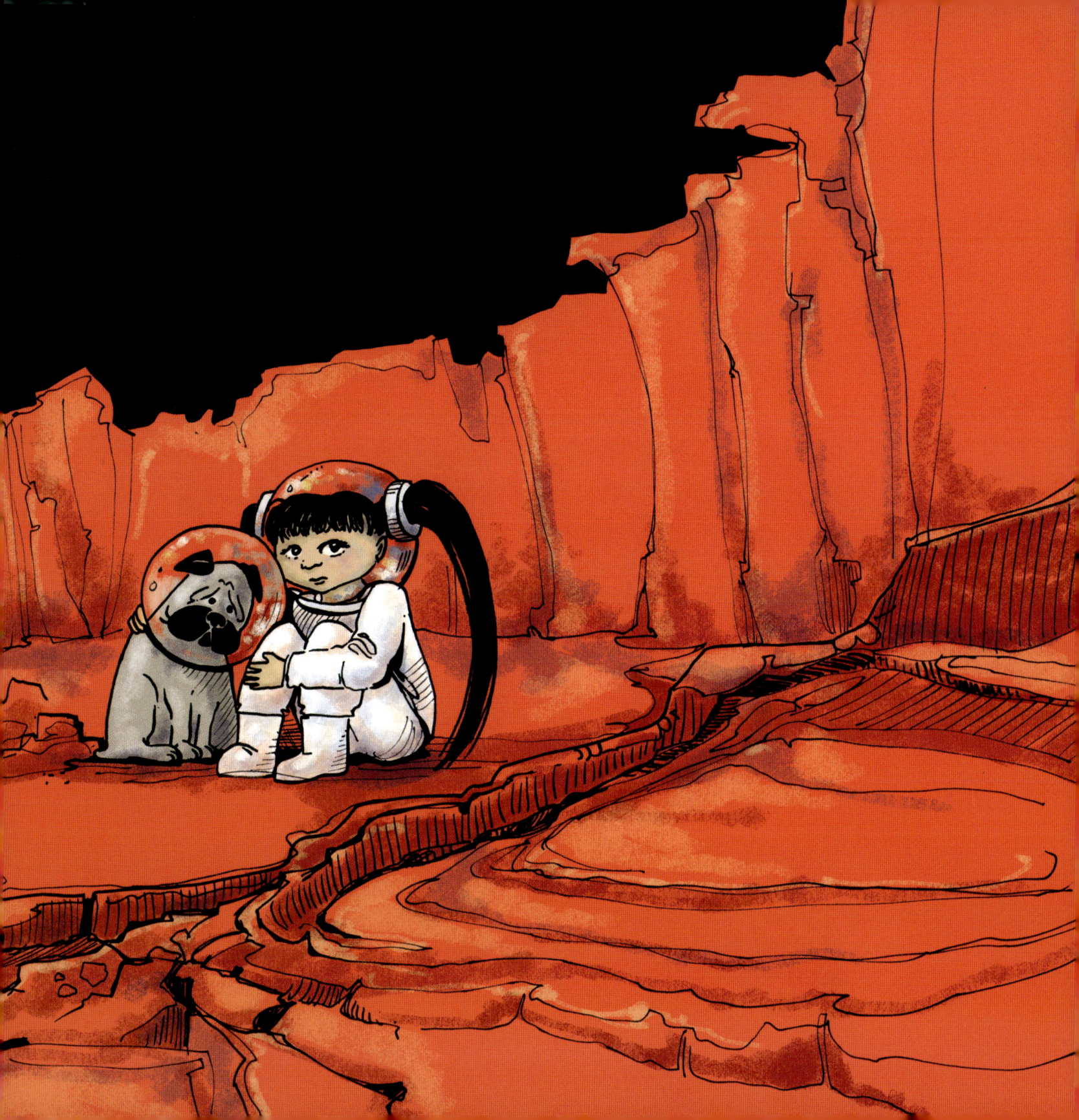

Ceres

Stella thought for a moment.
"How about the dwarf planet, Ceres? That could be a nice place to live."

Steve shook his head.
"There is no atmosphere on Ceres, and the gravity is so weak that you would float off into space and might hit a passing asteroid!"

"Jupiter it is, then," Stella said.
"It looks amazing."

Steve laughed.
"You wouldn't be able to stand on the surface! Jupiter is the biggest of all the planets. It's made of gas, and you would be sucked into the enormous storms in the great red spot and crushed by gravity!"

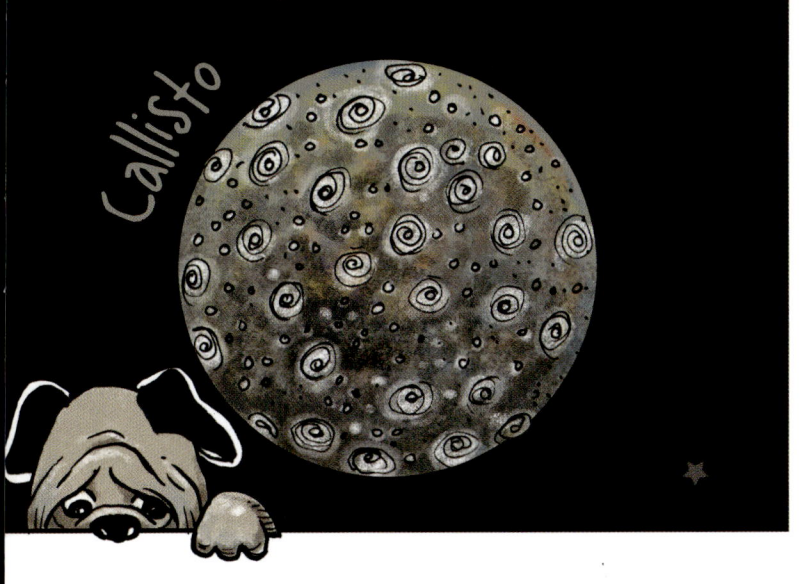

"What about one of Jupiter's moons?" Stella asked. "There are lots of them."

Steve chuckled. "You don't want to live on any of them. Io is volcanic. Europa has an icy surface and some believe life could be found underneath its crust. Ganymeade and Callisto are barren and cold, and made only of rock and ice. And all the other moons are too small!"

saturn

Stella thought some more.
"Saturn looks nice, Steve. Look at its fantastic rings. We could go skating!"

"Saturn, too, is big and made of gas, like Jupiter," Steve sighed. "And the rings aren't solid, but rather made of billions of chunks of ice and rock. Even I can't skate on them."

"Well, Saturn has lots of moons, too! I'm sure we could live on one of them," Stella replied.

"1. Mimas, 2. Tethys, 3. Rhea, 4. Dione, and 5. Iapetus are all cold and dead," said Steve.

Stella sighed. "Okay, so that leaves the dwarf planet Pluto. It's also cold and far from the sun."

"We've never been really close enough to Pluto to see what is there. It might look like this, but we don't really know at the moment. What I do know is that it is so far away and so cold that you would freeze the moment you got there," said Steve.

"What's out there,
even farther in space?" Stella asked.

"Beyond Pluto there are chunks of rock, small
dwarf planets, ice, and then interstellar space.
The next star would take thousands of years
for us to reach. Some people think there are more
stars in the galaxy than grains of sand in
the world. So who knows what is out there!"
said Steve.